Captain Amelia

B.E.N.

Morph

John Silver

Published by Hachette Partworks Ltd
ISBN: 978-1-906965-67-9
Date of Printing: December 2011
Printed in Singapore by Tien Wah Press

Disney

TREASURE PLANET

Disney

Hachette

"FIRE!"

Captain Nathaniel Flint stood on the deck of his
ship, shouting orders at his pirate crew to attack.
Now yet another merchant ship was at his mercy.
Flint's men boarded the ship and gathered up
its riches. Then, just as mysteriously as they had
appeared, the pirates vanished without a trace.

Years passed. Flint, the most feared pirate in the
galaxy, was no more. Yet his legend grew. Could
the stories be true? Had Flint hidden the loot of a
thousand worlds in a secret place? A place called...
Treasure Planet?

The tale of Flint's treasure had always thrilled young Jim Hawkins. As he guided his solar surfer above the sleepy town of Benbow on the Planet Montressor, Jim dreamed about finding Flint's legendary hoard.

But dreams were almost all Jim had. His father had left years ago. Jim's mother, Sarah, now ran the Benbow Inn all by herself. Things hadn't been easy for Jim or his mother.

One day, Jim went off by himself to sit on the roof of the inn. He didn't realise his life was about to change...

Suddenly, a spaceship crashed near the inn! Jim raced over to find a turtle-like alien called Billy Bones crawling out of the ship.

"He's after me chest! Ya gotta hide me, lad!" gasped Billy Bones. Jim helped the injured creature back to the inn.

Mrs. Hawkins and her good friend Dr. Doppler were shocked as Jim and Billy Bones stumbled through the door. "He's hurt bad. We gotta help him," Jim pleaded.

But sadly, nobody could help Billy Bones. He handed Jim a strange sphere. "He'll be comin' soon... can't let him find this," Bones whispered. Then, with his last gasp, he warned Jim: "Beware the cyborg!"

Suddenly, a rumbling sound outside drew Jim to the window. Pirates were heading for the inn!

"Quick! We gotta go!" exclaimed Jim. They all escaped through an attic window as the pirates stormed the inn.

As Jim, his mother and Doppler raced away in the doctor's carriage, Sarah looked back in horror as the pirates burned the inn to the ground.

When they arrived at Doppler's home, Jim
managed to open the sphere that Bones had given
him. Instantly, images of planets and stars filled
the room.

"Why, this appears to be some kind of map!" said
Dr. Doppler.

But it was no ordinary map. "Treasure Planet!"
Jim cried when he recognised the green, two-
ringed planet. The map showed the way to Flint's
legendary hiding place and its treasure!

Jim was eager to go. "With that treasure, we could rebuild the inn," Jim told his worried mother.

Doppler helped convince Sarah to let Jim go.

"I'll use my savings to hire a ship and crew," the doctor offered.

Reluctantly, Mrs. Hawkins finally agreed to let Jim go with Dr. Doppler to find the mysterious Treasure Planet.

A few days later, Jim and Dr. Doppler boarded the *RLS Legacy* – the ship that would take them to Treasure Planet. There, they met the tough and quick-witted Captain Amelia. She didn't trust the crew that Dr. Doppler had hired, and warned Jim and Doppler not to say anything about the map. Then she locked the map away in her private quarters.

"Young Hawkins will be working for our cook, Mr. Silver," Amelia explained to Dr. Doppler.

This decision made Jim very unhappy. And things were about to go from bad to worse. When Jim was escorted to the ship's galley, he saw the large figure of the cook standing at the stove...

"A cyborg!" Jim whispered to himself when he saw
that half of the cook's body was mechanical.

John Silver offered his hand. But remembering
Billy Bones' warning, Jim refused to shake hands
with Silver. "Jimbo! Now, don't be put off by this
hunka hardware," laughed the cook, rattling his
mechanical arm. Then Silver introduced Morph –
his playful, shape-shifting pet.

Once the ship had launched, Silver made another introduction. "Say hello to Mr. Mop and Mrs. Bucket," he told Jim.

At first, Jim did not like working for Silver. But over time, the cyborg taught Jim a lot about life on a ship – everything from peeling potatoes to tying knots.

Soon, Jim found himself growing fond of
John Silver. And Silver grew proud of the lad
as Jim showed signs of becoming a fine spacer.

"You got the makin's of greatness in ya!"
Silver told Jim. "But ya gotta take the helm
and chart yer own course. Stick to it, no
matter the squalls."

For Jim, Silver was like the father he'd
never had.

Then one morning, Jim overheard Silver and the crew planning to take over the ship and find the treasure themselves. Silver and the crew were really pirates!

One pirate accused Silver of being too close to Jim. "Methinks you have a soft spot for the boy."

"I care about one thing and one thing only... Flint's trove!" Silver announced to his crew.

Jim was crushed. But he knew he must warn Captain Amelia and Dr. Doppler.

Suddenly, a lookout on deck yelled out: "Planet ho!" Treasure Planet was finally in sight!

The pirates dashed on deck, but Silver went back to the galley – and saw Jim. One look told the pirate that Jim had overheard everything. Silver blocked the exit. Quickly, Jim jammed a pick into Silver's mechanical leg, surprising the old cyborg.

Jim raced to Captain Amelia's cabin.

Silver wasn't far behind. "Change in plans, lads!"
he bellowed to the pirates. "We move NOW!"

Captain Amelia acted swiftly when Jim barged into
her quarters and told her about Silver's plans. She
gave Jim the map. Then she, Jim, Morph and Dr.
Doppler escaped in one of the ship's longboats.

The pirates fired a cannon at the longboat, forcing it to crash land on Treasure Planet. Amelia was wounded, but she knew they could not rest because the pirates would be after them.

"We need a more defensible position, Mr. Hawkins – scout ahead," she ordered Jim. Jim and Morph headed off into the jungly landscape.

They hadn't gone far when a very confused robot
leapt out at Jim and hugged him.

"Sorry! But after a hundred years alone, you go
a little nuts!" said the robot, who was called B.E.N.
(Bio-Electronic Navigator).

B.E.N. had belonged to Captain Flint. But the
robot couldn't help them find the treasure because
Flint had removed part of his memory chip. All
B.E.N. could remember was that the treasure was in
the "centroid of the mechanism".

B.E.N. showed Jim his home, an ancient tower on a hill. It seemed a perfect spot to hide, so Jim brought Amelia and Doppler there.

Unfortunately, it wasn't long before Silver and his crew found them. The pirates captured Jim and his friends, and Silver took the map from Jim.

But Silver couldn't open the map. He demanded that Jim do it for him, but Jim refused.

"You want the map, you're taking me, too!" Jim insisted. Silver had no choice but to agree to bring Jim and the others along as they searched for the treasure.

 With Jim leading the way, the pirates and their
captives followed the path shown on the map.
Finally, they reached a cliff. There were strange
carvings and patterns on the ground, and Jim noticed
a place where the map fitted, like a key. As soon as
he inserted the map, a set of controls appeared.

 "Have mercy!" Silver whispered. As Jim pressed
the controls, a triangular portal of light opened in
front of them. Jim realised that the portal was a
doorway, and that he could make it open onto any
point in the galaxy.

 "So that's how Flint did it!" Jim said. He explained
how Captain Flint could go anywhere, steal treasure,
then disappear back through the portal.

"But where did he stash it all? Where's the blasted treasure?" asked Silver.

Jim remembered what B.E.N. had said about the treasure being in the centroid of the mechanism. So he set the portal to lead to the planet's core.

While Doppler and Amelia were held captive, the others entered the portal. There, the most amazing sight awaited them... the loot of a thousand worlds!

"Yeeeee-HAAAAAA!" the pirates yelled.

But Jim was more interested in Captain Flint's old pirate ship. Together with B.E.N., Jim sneaked aboard. The two stared in horror at what they found.

"C-C-Captain Flint?!" gasped the robot.

Perched on an old chair were the skeletal remains of Captain Flint! And B.E.N.'s missing memory chip was in his bony hand. Jim took the chip.

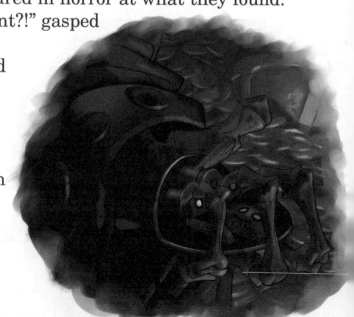

"Hold still, B.E.N.," said Jim as he plugged the chip into the robot's head. B.E.N. shuddered, then his face lit up in a huge smile.

"Whoa! Hello! It's all flooding back! All my memories! Flint pulled my memory circuit, so that I could never tell anyone about his... *booby trap*!"

Suddenly, the whole treasure chamber began to rumble and shake.

"Run, Jimmy!" cried B.E.N. Treasure Planet was about to explode! They had to get back through the portal and off the planet – fast.

"You go back and help the captain and Doppler," Jim told B.E.N. Then Jim desperately tried to get Flint's ship to start as the treasure chamber began to collapse. The pirates fled in wild panic... all except Silver.

Silver had followed Jim. When Jim finally got the ship started, he was amazed to see Silver on deck.

Silver realised that Flint's treasure-filled ship was all that could be saved from the chamber now. "Ah, Jimbo!" called Silver. "Aren't you the seventh wonder of the universe!"

Jim grabbed Flint's sword.

"Get back!" he yelled.

"I like ye, lad, but I've come too far to let you stand between me and me treasure," said Silver.

Just then, an explosion rocked the ship. Silver managed to grab hold of the ship with his mechanical arm, but Jim was hurled overboard!

Flint's ship was being pulled into the fiery core of Treasure Planet. Silver held on to the ship with all his strength. Suddenly, Morph flew up to him and pointed to Jim. The boy was clinging by one hand to the edge of a deep crevice!

Silver had to make a choice: he could either save the treasure – or Jim.

"Aaargh! Blast me for a fool!" exclaimed Silver. He truly cared about Jim and couldn't desert him now. Silver let go of the ship and caught Jim just in time.

Together, Jim, Silver and Morph made it back through the portal and onto the *Legacy*. Amelia, Doppler and B.E.N. had outwitted the panicked pirates and regained control of the ship.

"Hurry, people! We've got exactly two minutes and thirty-four seconds until the planet's destruction!" yelled B.E.N.

"We'll never get away in time!" shouted Doppler.

But Jim had an idea. If he could get back to the portal's controls, he could get it to open to another place in the galaxy. Sailing through the portal would bring them all to safety.

With Silver's help, Jim quickly created a makeshift solar surfer.

Jim surfed off the ship and
headed through the self-destructing
planet, straight for the control panel.
   The others steered the ship directly
into the triangle. With only seconds left,
Jim reached the controls and changed the
portal's destination!

As Treasure Planet exploded, the *Legacy* sailed through the portal to safety. Jim followed closely behind.

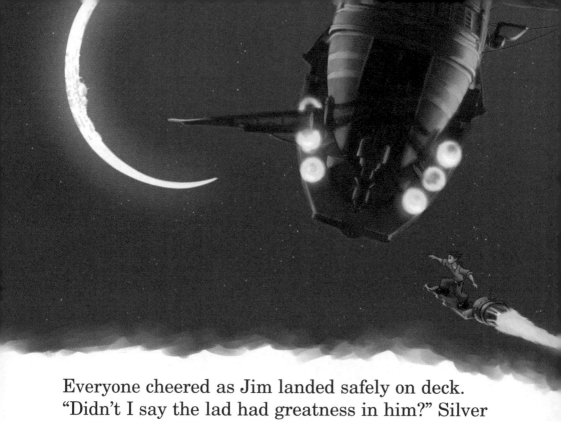

Everyone cheered as Jim landed safely on deck.

"Didn't I say the lad had greatness in him?" Silver shouted proudly.

"Unorthodox, but ludicrously effective," Amelia agreed. She even said that she would be happy to recommend Jim to the Interstellar Academy.

"Just wait until your mother hears about this!" exclaimed Dr. Doppler.

Jim turned to Silver, but the cyborg was gone.

Jim found Silver and Morph in the hangar bay, untying a longboat. Jim knew Silver had to leave to avoid going to prison, so Jim opened the hatch.

"What say ya ship out with us?" Silver asked.

Jim shook his head. Silver had taught him to believe in himself. Now he had his own dreams to pursue.

The old cyborg understood. "You're gonna rattle the stars, you are!" Then Silver handed Jim some treasure he'd managed to save. "For your dear mother, to rebuild that inn of hers," Silver explained.

Then, leaving Morph with Jim, the cyborg sailed out into space.

After rebuilding the Benbow Inn, Jim and his mother threw a party. Jim proudly wore the uniform of the Interstellar Academy. With a bright future ahead of him, Jim looked up gratefully at the stars. And there, he saw the glimmer of the pirate who had helped him find the greatest treasure of all – the treasure within himself.